GOOD-BYE, PAPA

GOOD-BYE, PAPA

Una Leavy

Illustrated by

Jennifer Eachus

Orchard Books
New York

for Paula
U.L.

for Joel and Jack
J.E.

Text copyright © 1996 by Una Leavy
Illustrations copyright © 1996 by Jennifer Eachus
First American Edition 1996 published by Orchard Books, New York
First published in Great Britain in 1996 by Orchard Books, London

Orchard Books
95 Madison Avenue
New York, NY 10016

Printed in Belgium
10 9 8 7 6 5 4 3 2 1

Library of Congress cataloging is available upon request.
ISBN 0-531-09545-2

In Papa's house the boys wake early.
Sun sneaks in the window.
Soft wind makes the curtains billow.
A bucket rattles.
"Who's coming to look for mushrooms?" Papa asks.

Over the fields they go—Shane and Peter and Papa.
Cocks crow; wisps of smoke curl up.
The boys run to keep up with Papa's step.
The mushrooms grow in cool dark nooks.
They pick them as quickly as they can.
"Mushrooms for breakfast," Papa says.
Nana fries them on the pan.

In Papa's garden the roses are in bloom.
It's hot this summer, and everywhere is dry.
"We have to water them," says Papa, "before the sun gets too high."

Now Papa makes a path.
He lays the slabs of red and gray beside the cabbage rows.
"I need cement," he says. "Let's go to town."
The boys hop in the car.
It isn't far, and Papa waves to everyone.

Shane and Peter wander round the shop.
There's lots to see—cement and tools and nails.
Then Papa says, "Who'd like some ice cream?"

Near Papa's house a lazy river flows.
Shane and Peter want to go to look for water hens.
There are none today, but Papa holds them tightly
to see swans gliding between the reeds.
In Papa's garden there's a hen run.
Six brown hens grumble and complain.
Shane and Peter bring in the eggs.

It's getting late; the stars are out.
It's almost time for bed.
Papa takes down the accordion.
Shane and Peter sit in their pajamas.
They drink their milk and listen while he plays.
He knows their favorite tunes and many more.
His hands fly in and out; his foot thumps on the floor.

Outside the moon hangs round and yellow.
As they lie in bed, scraps of music linger in their heads.
Good-night, Papa.

On Friday Shane and Peter have to go home.
Mom takes some photos.
The last thing they see is Papa's red T-shirt by the gate.
Good-bye, Papa. . . .

Some days later the phone rings.
It's Uncle Jim.
"Papa died this morning."

Next week they thank God for Papa's life.
Dad and his brothers carry Papa on their shoulders.
Shane and Peter put flowers on the grave.
Dad's crying.

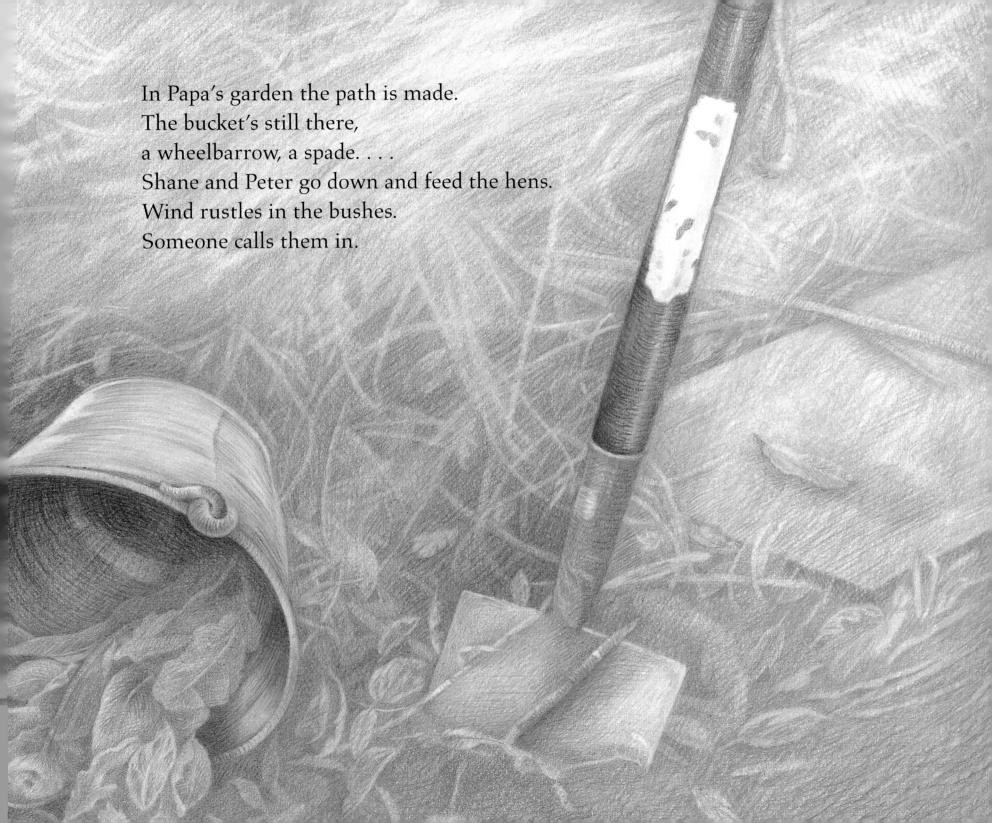

In Papa's garden the path is made.
The bucket's still there,
a wheelbarrow, a spade. . . .
Shane and Peter go down and feed the hens.
Wind rustles in the bushes.
Someone calls them in.

It's getting late; the stars are out.
It's almost time for bed.
They sit in their pajamas and drink milk.

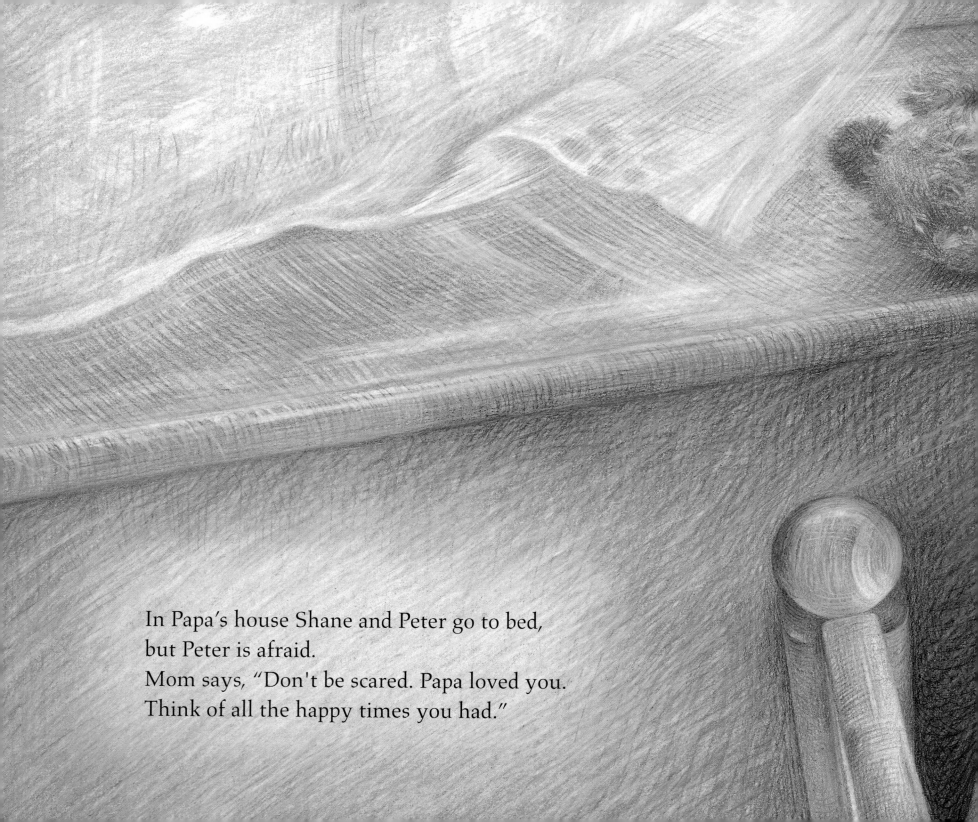

In Papa's house Shane and Peter go to bed,
but Peter is afraid.
Mom says, "Don't be scared. Papa loved you.
Think of all the happy times you had."

Outside the moon hangs round and yellow.
Soft wind makes the curtains billow.
Scraps of music linger in their heads. . . .